PEAS, PIRATES, *
AND OTHEl

Hatched and Nurtured by

Susie Senn
Jeanne-Marie Horsmann
Renney Senn

Illustrations by Christian G. Senn

PEAS, PIRATES, AND A POTATO BUG™
AND OTHER TEENSY TALES

We're happy we can share with you
This strange and cheeky brew.
And rest assured
That every word
Is absolutely true!

Table of Contents

Zoosense ~ 1

Twinkles ~ 3

Trouble ~ 7

Spikey ~ 9

Peas ~ 12

Pancakes 14

My Nose ~ 19

Toes ~ 21

Vegetables ~ 23

How Many ? ~27

Swizzle Sisters ~ 30

Rocks ~ 33

I Found It ~ 35

Spiders ~ 38

Footie Foodoodle ~ 40

Arthur ~ 45

Bunnies ~ 50

On My Belly ~ 52

Who Lives Here? ~55

The Pit ~ 58

Tummy Yummies ~ 61

Gangling Brocks ~63

What If? ~ 66

Pirates ~ 68

My Favorite Spot ~ 70

Black Banana ~ 73

Potato Bug ~ 75

Patty Puddles' Pots ~ 78

Billy O. Bumpkin ~ 80

A Frog Named Sam ~ 86

Scuttlebutt ~ 88

Curtain ~ 91

Zoosense

I went to the zoo and what did I see?
A very young monkey who looked just like me.

I went to the zoo and what did I hear?
The roar of a lion that seemed far too near.

I went to the zoo and what did I taste?
A big scoop of ice cream, not a drop did I waste.

I went to the zoo and what did I touch?
The drool of a rhino I didn't like much.

I went to the zoo and what did I smell?
The stink of manure that wasn't so swell.

I came from the zoo and what do you knowa?
I had so much fun I bought a pet boa!

Now all of a sudden it's dark and it's smelly.
How did I end up in my new pet's fat belly?

Twinkles

Twinkles gathered peanut shells
And stored them in his trunk.
This tiny baby elephant
Just liked to suck up junk.

He gathered almost everything,
Whatever he could find:
Rocks and sticks and candle wicks,
And food of any kind.

Small snails and leaves, he saved these too,
With candy and some goo.
Big bumblebees and chewing gum,
He stored these in there too.

He even sucked up beetle bugs
And wiggly little worms.
He must have had a trunk chock-full
Of icky little germs.

One day while he was trumpeting
His friends were all aghast,
When all at once he made a sneeze
That sounded like a blast.

His mama said, "Have you a cold,
My precious little son?
Please blow your nose to clear your head,
Then go and have some fun."

So Twinkles puffed himself right up,
And got his trunk all ready,
Then trumpeted a mighty blast
That made him quite unsteady.

And all that stuff packed in his trunk
Exploded in the air,
Then rained on down and all around
While causing quite a scare.

Now trunks are not for elephants
To save their special stuff;
No matter what they want to do
They just won't hold enough.

Showering, lifting, feeding, too,
Is what a snout's about,
It's not for storing junk inside,
Of this there is no doubt.

Young Twinkles learned this in a flash
With one almighty blow.
Important information for
An elephant to know!

Trouble

Again I am in trouble;
Deserved, I must confess.
My mother has it in for me,
She says I made a mess.

I took my sister's head off.
She asked for it, you see.
For when she passed me in the hall
She crossed her eyes at me.

I grabbed her by the hair
And yanked with all my might.
Uh oh, she simply came apart!
It really was a sight.

Her head rolled down the hallway
And thumped on down the stair,
Then kept on rolling out the door
And landed who cares where.

My mother went to pieces,
Beside herself with me.
She didn't like the mess I'd made
So here I sit you see . . .

She shut me in my bedroom,
Expecting me to whine,
But when she comes to let me out
My brother's next in line!

Spikey

Far out in the ocean
In the deep blue sea,
Lived a little puffer fish
As cute as he could be.

His parents called him Spikey -
A handsome little tyke -
A chubby little puffer fish,
Who was their true delight.

Now, looking big and tough
Is the goal of every puffer,
So bigger fish will swim away
And not eat them for supper.

Spikey and his friends
Would practice every day.
They'd blow up really big and fat.
How big? Well, who could say?

With cheeks and bodies bloated,
They looked like little balls,
Their tiny spikes and poppy eyes
Not looking fierce at all.

To be big and scary,
A threat was what they'd need.
Just then a big old fish swam by
Looking for some feed.

The fish saw Spikey as his lunch,
A yummy little meal.
He'd swallow him in one big gulp,
Then Spikey's gone for real.

When Spikey saw him coming
He puffed for all his worth,
'Til he was really big and fat
And twice his normal girth.

Spikey's eyes were huge,
His spikes looked long and sharp.
He seemed so big and oh so fierce
It made that fish depart.

"And none too soon," thought Spikey,
"I'm back to small and sleek."
It seems he'd huffed and puffed so hard
He'd sprung a great big leak!

Peas

Please tell me now, and don't you fib –
I know you wouldn't tease.
What if all my teeth were pulled
And then replaced with peas?

Could I suck a chocolate shake
Completely through a straw?
On an ear of golden corn,
Could I still munch and gnaw?

If my teeth were all pea green
Instead of pearly white,
When I made a great big grin
Would I just look a fright?

If I stuck my tongue way out
Amidst those little peas,
Would my friends all envy me
Or buzz off just like bees?

Tell me what you really think,
If you are so inclined.
I'd really like to go ahead
And book some dentist time.

If he pulled my pretty teeth
Replacing them with peas . . .
My gosh, it just now crossed my mind -
What happens if I *snEEZe*?

Pancakes

Renney just loved pancakes,
Of every shape and size
And if you saw how much he ate,
It'd be a big surprise.

He'd eat them for his breakfast
Before he went to school.
His mom would make them extra big,
And this he thought was cool.

He'd eat them by the plate load
And just when he was done,
He'd burp and sigh and ask for more.
Oh boy, oh boy, what fun!

One morning while awaiting
His normal pancake fare,
Renney started daydreaming
And had a vacant stare.

He thought about his pancakes,
What else with them to do?
Aha! He'd take a bunch to school;
His friends could have some too!

Renney knew his mom would think
That this was so not cool.
His pancakes were for him alone
And not for friends at school.

But Renney didn't listen
To what she thought was right.
He chose to do it anyway
And hid them out of sight.

He took his little lunch pail
And snuck a few inside,
Then shut the lid and snapped the lock,
Smiling side to side.

He had some extra pockets.
He stuffed some in there, too.
He even stuffed some in his pants.
His mother never knew.

Then he waddled off to school
With all his pancakes hidden.
He felt so smug and smart inside
To do something forbidden.

But Renney hadn't planned it,
And didn't have much luck,
When all the pancakes in his pants
Began to turn to muck.

His teacher called on Renney
To come up to the board
And show the class what he had learned,
A task he just abhorred.

Facing all his classmates,
He felt the pancakes slide
Right down his legs into his shoes
And this he couldn't hide.

He felt the butter seep,
The sticky syrup too,
Out through his pants for all to see.
Oh now what would he do?

Then he heard a sound
That no one else could hear,
His mother's voice was calling him
Resounding in each ear:

17

"Renney! You've been daydreaming!
Your breakfast's getting cool.
Just finish up, and wash your plate,
You need to get to school!"

Renney felt relieved
He wasn't caught at school,
With pancakes oozing everywhere
And looking like a fool.

But then he felt a lump
And soon became aware
There was some butter in his drawers.
Now how did that get there?

My Nose

My nose fell off the other night
And landed in the stew.
My mom was looking elsewhere
And so didn't have a clue.

She never even noticed
That my nose was in the pot.
It hurt so bad I had to wail,
"My nose is boiling hot!"

Completely unaware she said,
"Dear Johnny, have some stew.
I used some great ingredients,
Especially for you."

She put some stew into my bowl
And yes, I was appalled.
But then I dared to take a taste,
She's mother after all.

Instantly I knew it needed something -
Maybe sugar?
The salty taste was clearly from
A big ol' gnarly booger!

Toes

I feel so sorry for our toes;
We put them through such use.
By going barefoot everywhere
They take so much abuse.

To start, we step on rocks and bugs
And bump them into things.
I'm sure that if they had a thought
They'd wish that we had wings.

We kick at cans and soccer balls;
Why don't our toes protest?
To put on shoes, they well could ask,
Is that a big request?

At times big horses step on them
And squish our toes quite flat.
On top of all their other woes,
What must they think of that?

With all the things we do to them
They seldom make a fuss.
You'd think our toes would want to stay
A mile away from us!

Vegetables

Susie's mother always told her
She'd grow up big and strong.
If she would eat her vegetables,
There's no way she'd go wrong.

But Susie hated vegetables;
Each tasted like the other,
And every night at dinner
She'd hide them from her mother.

The cupboard was a special place
To hide her lima beans.
And when there wasn't one inch left,
She'd stuff them in her jeans.

Brussels sprouts, and beets, and squash,
They tasted just as bad.
And when she got them off her plate
She sure felt mighty glad.

In every nook and cranny
The vegetables would go;
It made no difference, big or small,
Or even high or low.

The potted plants had lots of dirt
To bury stuff just right,
Where broccoli and cauliflower
Stayed hidden out of sight.

Without a single vegetable,
Susie grew no taller.
It was indeed a troubling fact
She kept on getting smaller.

Each day that passed saw Susie shrink.
It simply wasn't fair.
Until one day she barely was
A spot upon her chair.

Now Susie finally realized
Her mother wasn't wrong.
If she would eat her vegetables,
She'd grow up big and strong.

So Susie ate her vegetables
And cleaned up every plate.
She ate so much her tummy ached,
And soon she put on weight.

Susie grew some more each day
'Till she was plump and sassy,
A roly-poly jolly thing,
Quite wide and awfully gassy.

Her appetite for vegetables
By now could not be stopped.
She ate and ate and ate some more
Until she finally popped!

How Many?

How many grains
Of sand can there be
On top of the dunes
And down to the sea?

I really must know
But whom should I ask?
Should I start with the starfish
And give them the task?

Or maybe the clams
Can count as they hide
All the pieces of sand
Washed around by the tide.

Sand dollars might know,
But no answer they'll give;
This secret they'll keep
For as long as they live.

Maybe the crabs
Can give it a try
And add it all up
Ere the day has gone by.

Or better yet birds
Can count as they soar
And add up the grains
Since they see so much more.

Who then can tell me?
I don't know who yet,
But thank them I will
And I'll owe them a debt.

Then once I find out
How many grains there can be,
I think I will count
All the
drops
in
the
sea!

The Swizzle Sisters' Birthday Party

The Swizzle sisters sang off-key
And played two violins,
While dancing on their birthday cake
Atop two zeppelins.

Invited were their closest friends -
They came from everywhere;
Some hopped, some flew or came by boat,
Who knows how some got there?

A chicken wore his cowboy boots
And rode a painted pony.
A meerkat donned a party hat
Of crabgrass and baloney.

A pigeon blew the flugelhorn,
Some pigs played roly-poly,
Two hippos danced on tippy toe
While eating macaroni.

An otter played a big bass drum,
Four toads ate lots of prunes,
A bullfrog rode a whirligig
While balancing six spoons.

A monkey played a toy kazoo,
A walrus juggled plates,
Three penguins sped around and 'round
On shiny roller skates.

Some lizards danced the bunny hop,
Two spiders knitted noodles,
And all the while a poodle dog
Jumped up and down on strudels.

"It's time to light our birthday cake!"
The Swizzle Sisters goaded,
So someone lit a great big match
And the whole weird mess exploded!

Rocks

I found some small rocks
And painted them red.
They're under the pillow
At the head of my bed.

I found some big rocks
And painted them yellow.
Oops, right through the window –
Oh wow did dad bellow!

I found some rough rocks
And painted them blue.
I put them inside
My mother's old shoe.

I found some smooth rocks
And painted them brown,
Then went to the toilet
And flushed them all down.

Now that I've painted
Every rock I can find,
What's left to paint?
I must make up my mind.

Painted rocks in mom's shoe,
In our house and my bed . . .
I've got it! I'll paint
All the rocks in my head!

I Found It

I found it in a muddy hole.
I found it buried deep.
It took a while to dig it out
But now it's mine to keep.

Its color has a hint of blue
That shifts to brownish black.
It's darker on the top and sides
Than on the front and back.

It has an odor, that I'm sure,
Of what it's hard to tell.
I hold it close and take a whiff -
Oh what a dreadful smell!

I think I've found a mushy part,
When poked it starts to ooze.
My sister says, "Get rid of it.
We haven't time to lose!"

My brother will not play with it.
He looks on with alarm.
I do not know just why this is -
I think it has great charm.

My cousin asked to see it close
But when it made a quack,
A funny look came on his face.
He quickly gave it back.

To have some fun there is no place
To which my thoughts won't stoop.
Imagine what my mom'll do
When she finds it in her soup!

Spiders

I love my little spiders.
They're really good not bad.
My brother wants to step on them;
This makes me really mad.

He catches big and little ones.
He gives them no excuses.
I try to find them first because
They have so many uses.

They rid the house of insects -
Like flies and other pests.
I let the little spiders in
To eat unwanted guests.

Though dusting is so boring,
The spiders help me do it.
I wave around a spider's web,
The dust then sticks right to it.

Spiders are so helpful.
My brother's such a dope.
I thought he'd see them more like me;
There really is no hope.

So come to me, my crawlies,
And join with one another.
The time has finally come, you see,
For eating up my brother!

Footie Foodoodle

This the story of
Footie Foodoodle,
A long fat green foot
With a head like a noodle.

His noodle could stretch
So far up in the sky
He could look over mountains,
No matter how high.

The day came when Footie
Decided to claim
His one truest sweetheart,
Fee Fee by name.

He put on his finest –
His hat and his vest –
Then set out to find her,
But where? was the test.

"Oh where is my Fee Fee?"
He asked with a shrug.
"I'll search 'till I find her,
Then give her a hug.

With her fat little toes
And long noodle head
I've decided to woo her
And ask her to wed."

So Footie's long noodle
Stretched up very high -
He knew he'd find Fee Fee
If he looked from the sky.

He saw her below him
Dressed all in pure white,
With her pink polished toenails –
A beautiful sight!

Her long noodle head
Was so covered in bows
They cascaded in garlands
Right down to her toes.

Her lips were like rosebuds,
Her cheeks powdered pink,
This rainbow of color
Made Footie's eyes blink.

Soon Fee Fee and Footie
Were happily wed.
"What a handsome young couple,"
The villagers said.

And living together
As husband and wife,
They could both see before them
A wonderful life.

Weeks passed when Fee Fee
Soon started detecting
A bulge in her ankle
That showed her expecting.

A new little footie
Was now on its way,
Just how long and how pretty,
Well, no one could say.

Not many months later
Sweet Fee Fee gave birth
To a mystery baby
Not quite of this earth.

For Footie and Fee Fee
Could not understand
How they ended up having
A thirteen pound hand.

Arthur

Arthur loved all kinds of sounds,
Loud, soft, both far and near.
He'd cup his hands up to his ears
To see what he could hear.

He ran up to the far North Pole
To listen to the whales,
And then down to the southern pole
To hear the icy gales.

He crept into the baby's room
To listen to her cry,
And then next to the kitchen stove
To hear the bacon fry.

He rushed up hills to hear the geese,
Some honking overhead.
He raced to farms to hear the lambs
All bleating to be fed.

Though Arthur ran so far and fast
It really was for naught.
He simply couldn't keep this up,
But then he had a thought.

"I think I know just what to do.
I'm clever as a fox.
I'll gather all the sounds there are
And keep them in a box!

"By doing this I'll always have
All my sounds at hand.
With all of them accessible
To hear each on demand."

So Arthur raced around the world
Collecting every noise,
Then threw them in a great big box
As if they were his toys.

But now that all the sounds were kept
So hidden deep away,
The world was silent as a tomb
With nothing left to say.

When Arthur looked outside he saw
A robin on the wing,
But not a chirp came from its throat
With no notes left to sing.

Soon Arthur found he missed them all
And couldn't even sleep,
With nothing left to listen to,
Not even one small peep.

So Arthur took his box of sounds
And cast them far and wide.
But no matter what he tried,
One still remained inside.

He shook the box one final time.
Oh rats! It blew apart!
For Arthur's final sound had been
A supersonic fart!

49

Bunnies

I have a bunch of bunnies
That live inside my house.
They really do not bother me;
They're quiet as a mouse.

I find them in the corners.
I find them on the stairs.
I find them under writing desks
And even under chairs.

They show up without warning,
As many bunnies do;
I turn my back on just a pair
And then have twenty-two.

I always find the new ones
In places I ignore,
Like corners of my dressing room
Or just behind the door.

I throw them out while cleaning;
It's such an endless chore.
For every one that I discard
I soon have twenty more.

I never ever feed them –
I know you think I must –
But these are not the furry kind;
They're all made out of dust!

On My Belly

I lie on my belly
Just looking around.
There's a lot to be seen
Down here on the ground.

There's a very large bug -
It's a beetle, I think -
With its rear in the air
It makes quite a stink.

Over there is a worm,
So squirmy and slimy.
If I look at it closer,
I see it's quite grimy.

Underneath a small leaf,
When I look oh so closely,
I see a small bug
That's translucent and ghostly.

Climbing up in the grass
I can see a black ant
That holds in its jaws
A piece of a plant.

But wait, what is this
Moving next to my cheek?
It's a caterpillar whose nose
Looks like a small beak.

And crawling behind it
In front of my nose
Is a millipede whose feet
Must have thousands of toes.

I'd love to be free
To keep having my fun,
But mom fears the worst
For her curious son.

She's convinced awful monsters
Live out in our lawn,
And before she could save me
Her son would be gone.

If she knew what I've done,
I know she'd drop dead,
'Cause I've brought them all home
To live in my bed!

Who Lives Here?

There is a hole that I have found
High up in a tree.
Each morning I look up at it
And wonder what I'll see.

It's so far above the ground
It's hard to see inside,
But I know there's an open space
Where anything can hide.

Could it be that it's a home
To a fluffy sharp-eyed owl?
Or maybe it's a cozy den
For wayward barnyard fowl.

Perhaps the hole could hide a mouse
That's surely lost its way;
Or a charm of hummingbirds –
A perfect place to stay!

A little squirrel could nestle there,
Snuggled in so tight;
A family full of baby bats
Would all fit in just right.

Someday I think I'll take a stool
And climb up there to see
All the creatures living there
Whatever they might be . . .

On second thought this just might be
A big and stupid blunder.
What if there's a zombie there
Or something worse, I wonder?

The thing might eat me all at once -
Or gosh - just bit by bit.
What if it tries to gulp me down
And I'm too big to fit?

I nearly made a big mistake
And paid an awful toll.
All because of wondering
What's in that silly hole.

The Pit

When Chris was just a little boy
He seemed to cast a spell.
At first his parents blamed his toys
For a very stinky smell.

They couldn't imagine what it was
That caused this awful stink;
It was so strong around their son
It forced them both to blink.

They cleaned his clothes and washed his hair
And checked between his toes.
Still all their friends would stop and stare,
Then quickly hold their nose.

His mother put him in a tub
And washed him head to toe.
Despite how much she rubbed and scrubbed
The stink refused to go.

The smell got worse as time went by;
His mother said it shocked her.
His father had enough and cried,
"Let's take him to the doctor!"

Then Chris did something very odd . . .
His eyes grew wide with wonder.
He made a jerky little nod
And then a sound like thunder.

It was a most amazing sneeze –
It rated more than ten.
It even caused a startling breeze
As strong as who knows when.

And from his nose a strange thing flew,
Quite green and kind of hairy.
The source of Chris' strange pee-u?
The pit from some old cherry!

Tummy Yummies

Witches jowls
Goblin scowls
Wings of bats
Sewer rats
Drool of snakes
Lizard cakes
Slimy worms
Things that squirm
'Possum tails
Dragon scales
Pumpkin goo
Dirty shoe
Let them brew
In a stew.
Drink a cup.
Throw it up!

Gangling Brocks

This was to be a magic day,
A wonder to my mind.
I'd hike through fields and hills until
I'd find a wondrous find.

'Round about the meadow
And over through the trees
I thought I spied some gangling brocks
Playing in the breeze.

You never see a gangling brock -
They must come out at night.
The mystery no one understands
Is why they shun the light.

They darted hither and thither,
Up and over and yon;
First here, then there, oh everywhere,
Way back and then beyond.

Their play was just like lightning,
Fast and sharp and quick,
With loop de loops and spirals, too.
It all was quite a trick.

They zipped and flipped and fluttered,
Showing off as if to say,
"We're really not at all like this.
This is your special day."

I saw them in the sunlight,
All furry, brown and shiny.
From where I was, so far away,
They looked quite dark and tiny.

So then I crept up closer -
As close as I could get -
To then see what would happen when
The sun began to set.

And as the light began to fade
They flew in close formation.
But what is this? I think I see
A sudden transformation.

All at once I realized,
It hit me just like that.
It seems my brilliant gangling brocks
Were just a bunch of bats!

What If?

What if my feet had fingers?
What if my hands had toes?
What if my elbow grew out of my face?
What would I do with my nose?

What if my cat sang opera?
What if my dog could cook?
What if my goldfish watched TV all day
And never opened a book?

What if my eggs were purple?
What if my bread were green?
What if my cheese walked off of my plate
Never again to be seen?

What if the stars moved backwards?
What if the moon wore clothes?
What if the world just flipped upside down?
Would my hair now smell like my toes?

Pirates

Avast, me hardies, listen well!
I'm here and mighty bold.
So don't ye whine or make a fuss;
I've come to steal yer gold.

I am the captain of this ship -
Infamous One-eyed Jack.
And when I steal yer pretty gems,
You'll never get 'em back!

My pirates are the meanest men
To sail the seven seas.
They'll take yer trinkets and yer gold
In spite of all yer pleas.

Abandon hope, ye salty dogs.
Sit still, this won't take long.
For all yer great and fancy jewels
To me they now belong.

Don't ever try to hide yer rings,
For if I'm forced to linger,
I'll keep yer hand, but to be fair,
I'll give ye back yer finger.

So if ye see us coming round,
Heave to, but have no dread.
Just give me all yer gold doubloons -
I'll let ye keep yer head!

My Favorite Spot

Around the corner, down the hill,
You'll find my favorite spot.
It is the place where I can go
And be what I am not.

It's by a big old crooked tree,
That's magic it would seem.
It's here I sit and lose myself
And travel in a dream.

For when I'm here, I'm in a world
Without a single care.
My thoughts are magic vehicles
That take me anywhere.

I've often been a meteor,
Shooting 'cross the sky.
I've swung around the earth and moon
And watched the days pass by.

One day I was a mighty ant
And through the grass I'd go.
I carried loads of such a size
It really was a show.

I've been a dolphin, oh so sleek,
Swimming in the sea.
I played with seals and slithery eels;
It was a sight to see.

Today I think I'll be a bear,
Just lazing in the sun.
The animals will see me there,
And scared to death, they'll run.

Tomorrow is another day;
Perhaps I'll be a bird.
On second thought, oh what the heck,
I think I'll be a turd!

Black Banana

I have a black banana.
It sits upon a shelf.
"Whatever shall I do with it?"
I have to ask myself.

My sister sure could use it;
She likes them soft and mushy.
She'll add it to some ice and milk,
And then she'll have a slushy.

My mother just might take it
And put it by her glass.
She'll eat it with her oats and bran,
But it will give her gas.

Give it to the baby?
You know just what he'll do.
He'll mash it in the carpeting
And mix it with his poo!

Maybe I'll just leave it
To shrivel while it lingers,
Then save some more for Halloween;
What perfect witches' fingers!

Potato Bug

My brother has a mouse.
My sister has a toad.
I just found a potato bug
As I walked down the road.

I handled him with care.
He was so very small.
He also was so delicate,
Just barely there at all.

But as I stopped to think
About my little pet,
I wondered how I'd keep him safe
And soon began to fret.

What about a box?
I wonder what he eats?
Perhaps he'd like some snails and grass . . .
Would he eat my beets?

Will my mother like him?
(My brother has the mouse.)
Will my new potato bug
Be welcome in our house?

So I thought what trouble.
I'd better put him back.
My mom will shriek "*POTATO BUG!*"
And have a yuck attack.

All at once it hit me.
It happened just like that.
I'll give my mom another choice -
A fluffy little cat.

What a great idea!
A kitty is so sweet.
And if I train my pet just right,
I've eaten my last beet!

Patty Puddles' Pots

Patty Puddles potted plants;
In puddles Patty plotted.
Putting plants in pretty pots
Made Patty Puddles potted.

Patty's pal is Polly.
Polly's plants are few.
Polly put her plants in puddles;
Patty's potty too.

Polly planted peppers,
Put in Patty's pots.
When Patty peed, poor Polly panged
And tied herself in knots.

Posey's Polly's planting pal,
Patty Puddles' too.
Posey put her pepper pots
In Patty Puddles' shoe.

Patty's pals put potted palms
On pallets placed by Posey.
While Patty's precious porky pig
Oinked "Pig Around the Posies."

This plethora of potting pals
Put Patty in a panic.
She piddled in a pepper pot
And popped right off the planet!

Billy O. Bumpkin

Billy O. Bumpkin
Was very unkind.
He'd hurt people's feelings
And not even mind.

He'd start in the morning
With sweet sister Gert,
Then tease his two brothers,
Tommy and Bert.

His parents had warned him
It hurts to be teased,
But Billy O. Bumpkin
Did just as he pleased.

He'd pull Gertie's pigtails,
And then call her names,
And hide Tommy's baseballs
And Bert's army games.

But something occurred
Very late one dark night
Not long after Billy
Had turned off his light.

He snuggled between his
Soft sheets with a sigh
And then fell asleep
In the blink of an eye.

Suddenly Billy
Got a terrible fright.
He dreamed that he saw
A most horrible sight.

His body was now
A fat warty old toad,
Hopping and croaking down
A dark creepy road.

He hadn't hopped far
When he heard a loud sound
That warned him "Watch out!"
Someone else was around.

It was a mean little kid –
Just about eight -
Who'd trap many toads
And would use them as bait.

He'd grab them and squeeze them
And give them a poke,
Then chuckle out loud
At his cruel little joke.

The toads would start squirming
When tied to his line,
Which took only seconds,
A very short time.

For this was the way
He caught all of his fish,
Then eat them for dinner
Plopped down on a dish.

He scooped Billy up
And into his pocket,
Then ran down the road
As fast as a rocket.

"Oh boy, this is great!"
The boy yelled with zeal.
Then stopped at the lake
As he pulled out his reel.

But when he sat down
To prepare his new bait,
Poor Billy got scared
As he thought of his fate.

He tried to yell out,
"This isn't a joke!"
But all that came out
Of his mouth was a croak.

He wriggled and squirmed
Many times in alarm
While hoping past hope that
He'd come to no harm.

As his small body
Was cast in the lake,
He croaked out so loudly,
He startled awake.

He sat up in bed
And heaved a big sigh,
Soon saw where he was,
Then wailed out this cry:

"I really came close
To the end of my road.
How could I have been
Such a terrible toad?

I finally know now that
My teasing is bad,
And only makes people
Feel awful and sad."

So after that dream
Billy mended his ways,
And was a good brother
For the rest of his days.

But a curious price
Billy paid to be wise.
From that day to this
He eats nothing but flies!

A Frog Named Sam

Written by Chris, age 5

Once upon a time
There was a boy named Chris
And he had a pet frog named Sam
And Sam was in a box and he croaked.

~ The End ~

What the public is saying about
PEAS, PIRATES, AND A POTATO BUG™

"Two toes way up!"
Footie Foodoodle

"This book should be rated AAARRR."
One-Eyed Jack

"No way I'd ever eat a beet!"
Potato Bug

"This book's a blast!"
The Swizzle Sisters

"I can't believe I ate the whole thing."
Pancake Kid

"What a gas!"
Veggie Girl

"Will leave you with peas envy!"
The Reluctant Dentist

"Oh boy, this is great!"
Mean Little Kid

"THAT was in my nose?!"
Chris

88

*"Reading this book gives us
the warm fuzzies."*
The Dust Bunnies

"Yummy!"
Black Banana

*"When I read Peas
I thought I would burst!"*
Spikey

*"Peas, Pirates, and a Potato Bug is nothing to
sneeze at!"*
Twinkles

"Ribbit!"
Sam, the frog

*"Peas, Pirates, and a Potato Bug –
Perfect!"*
Patty, Polly and Posey

"I gulped it all down!"
Hungry Boa

~ ~ ~

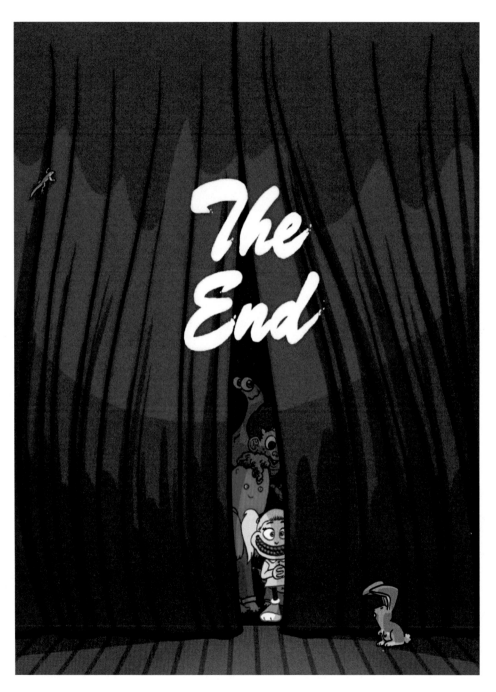

Made in the USA
San Bernardino, CA
11 August 2018